To: M°Kenzie

Happy 6th BIRthday Enjoy

Dantlynne Moss

To my Incredible Family and all my Friends,
Thank you for the gift of your friendship and your love.
Thank you for supporting me and believing in me.
Thank you for listening to my dreams, nurturing them and cheering me on along the way.
Thank you for sharing yourselves with me, letting me do the same, and for being such an important part of my life.

You are all like the beautiful snowflakes that CiCi and Ace watch from their window...each special, each unique, one-of-a-kind and each able to shimmer in your own way. And, like that first perfect snow, you have all added to the beauty and richness of my life.

To all the Children in our Wonderful World,
Thank you for helping us to remember how good it feels to share with a friend, to hold hands, to really laugh out loud, to dream, to see the world through your eyes and to believe.
Thank you for sharing your wonder of the world with all us "big kids," who sometimes forget.
Thank you for explaining how the world really works and what really matters.
Thank you for allowing us to get a refresher course while "teaching" you.
Thank you for the many gifts you so freely give: your magic and belief in all the possibilities, your songs and stories that all end in exclamation points, your smiles and laughter that twinkle in your eyes, your sheer delight in the smallest things, your joy and all your other precious gifts!

To Alex (Karin's kitty) and Jazz the DreamDog (my magic doggie) and all the other "Four-legged Children" of the world,
Thank you for the gift of unconditional love. Your gentle presence adds so much to our lives.

I Love You All, Rainey

Produced Exclusively for
The Children's Place
by DreamDog Press
3686 King Street, Suite 160
Alexandria, VA 22302

Order online @ **childrensplace.com**

Copyright © 2004 The Children's Place
Created and Written by Rainey (Lorraine Lee Friedman)
Illustrated by Karin Huggens
Graphic Design, Type Treatment and Cover Layout by Zenon Slawinski

Cataloging-in-Publication Data
Rainey (aka Friedman, Lorraine Lee.)
The Greatest Gift by Rainey; illustrated by Karin Huggens – 1st ed.
p.cm.
SUMMARY: CiCi and Ace want to give something to all the special people in their lives to say "thank you." They come up with a creative way to show everyone how much they care and realize that the greatest gift is giving to others. Included is a Sing-Along Music CD with original songs, a Note for Families about the value of teaching your children to give to others, and a Family Art Activity.

ISBN: 0-9666199-3-5
1. Discovery and learning – Juvenile Fiction. 2. Brother and sister adventure -- Juvenile Fiction.
3. Learning the greatest gift is giving to others–Juvenile Fiction. 4. Season of Giving– Juvenile Fiction.
I. Huggens, Karin II.Title

The GREATEST Gift

by

⭐ Rainey

Illustrated by
Karin Huggens

Our story begins one really cold day
at the start of the winter holiday.

CiCi and Ace were waiting for the first snow
when a super strong wind started to blow.

They looked out the window at the night sky
and saw bright little flakes shimmering by.

CiCi called, "It's snowing! It's snowing! Come and see!"
It was beautiful to watch with her whole family.

Ace started planning all the things he would do.
"I want to make a snowman – oh – and a fort, too."

CiCi said, "What about a whole snow family?
We could build a Mom, Dad, baby, you and me."
Mom brought in hot chocolate as they watched it snow,
all huddled together, near the front window.

Then Ace and CiCi made up a song that was all the rage and performed it right there, on their living room stage.

They held their hands *up* with little shakes pretending that they were big snowflakes.

And even their Mom and Dad got in the groove
when their baby sister Violet started to move.

She was trying to do their snowflake dance
and had a wide-eyed look like she was entranced

Mom said, "Okay, little snowflakes, tomorrow's a big day.
But, now it's time to go to bed.
Let's start heading that way."

That night, CiCi and Ace both had *snowflake dreams*.
CiCi was a *snow fairy floating on moonbeams*.

Ace woke up with a smile on his face;
"Hey CiCi – I just won the snowflake race!

Each snowflake had an engine that motored it down,
and mine was the first one to make it to the ground."

They dressed up warmly for their snowy day
and went outside with their friends to play.

CiCi and Mae had an idea: "Let's get the boys now!"
They snuck up with their hands full of snow,
took aim — KAPOW!!

In a blizzard snow battle, they fought really well.
Who won? They were all wet, so it was hard to tell.

They all giggled and laughed until it was late
and time to end their snowy play date.

CiCi hugged Mae good-bye then Mae started to go.
"You're my best friend," she called,
"just thought you should know."

Mae called back,
"CiCi, you're my very best friend, too!
We have so much fun together, whatever we do."

That night when CiCi and Ace went to bed,
an idea  popped into CiCi's head.

"I want to give
presents to our family,
neighbors and friends,
teachers and mailman...
my list never ends.

There are so many people that I want to thank,
but I don't have enough money,"
she shook her piggy bank.

"Hey, CiCi, that's a great idea. I have a long list, too.
Together we can figure out something we can do.

Mom always says giving comes from the heart.
And Dad says that's the best place to start."

"How about cookies?" CiCi was thinking of food.
"Chocolate chippers always put me in a good mood."

"Yea," Ace answered, "but everyone likes a different kind.
We'd be baking zillions of cookies," he saw it in his mind.

"Okay," CiCi said, "let's think of some way to share all of our feelings and show how much we care."

Ace agreed, "One special thing about this time of year is how it makes the important things seem really clear. We can make cards! That's a good way to tell everyone how we feel today."

Their plan was to start as a new day was dawning.
They both hopped out of bed while Ace was still yawning.

They *painted* and drew cards for most of the day
writing the messages they wanted to say.

They thanked their friends for being sweet,
their neighbors for being nice,
and on their grandparents' cards
they wrote, "We should thank you twice."

They thanked their teachers
for teaching them all kinds of things
and decorated those cards with ribbons and strings.
The card for their parents was of a family made of snow
that said, "You are in our hearts, wherever we go."

All afternoon, they delivered their cards
walking through the snow
to friends' and neighbors' yards.

And all day they got back gifts of hugs and smiles
and learned that giving seems to go on for miles.

That night when CiCi got into bed,
she felt something beside her poking her head.
She reached over to see and a smile lit her face.
There was a card from her big brother Ace.

On the card was a picture that he drew
of him with his little sister, just those two.
Inside was a message as if he had kissed her
that said, "You are the Very Best Little Sister."

At about the same time, Ace climbed into bed,
put his feet on the ladder, but found a card there instead.

First one side of his mouth turned up
and then the other when he read that his card said,
"You're the Best Big Brother."

They giggled as they hugged then had a tickle fight.
As snow fell outside, they said,

"I love you"
and turned out the light.

They learned that giving isn't only
about buying presents and things,

but about sharing
the LOVE and JOY that TRUE GIVING brings.

Giving From The Heart...with Our Children

This time of year is definitely "the season of giving," but for many children it is also the season of "I want..." This year, switch the focus from what they want to receive to what they can give. Talk with your children about the true joy of giving to others. Here are some steps we can all take to embrace the giving spirit all year round:

- **Point out the effects of your children's giving behaviors.** Help them realize and notice the positive results of giving. Say something when they share toys, treats or anything else to make them aware of the effect of their giving: "Remember when you shared your snacks on the playground and gave some to Eva? It really made her happy. Did you notice her smile?"

- **Praise your children's caring behavior.** When you see your children engaging in caring, giving behaviors, tell them how proud you are of them: "It was so nice of you to include Jamal in your game. He looked like he was really having fun. You're a good friend." This helps your children know that you value kindness as much as their other achievements.

- **Encourage caring comments.** When children say nice things about a friend or even a character in a book or on a TV show, engage them in these discussions, even if the objects of their caring are make-believe characters. If encouraged, they will use these same comments and direct them towards others. Caring *about* others leads to caring *for* and giving *to* others.

- **Teach and practice appreciation when someone gives something to your children.** The "magic words" we all learned as children still hold a lot of power. When your children are taught to say "thank you" when someone does something nice for them, they are learning the value of gratitude. A little note saying thank you for a present, even if they just draw a picture, teaches them the importance of acknowledging the nice things that others do. When you say "please" and "thank you," you are setting a good example for your children.

- **Do family giving projects.** A good way to start would be at the beginning of the school year by donating supplies to backpack programs for homeless children. In the winter, donate used coats, gloves and hats that no longer fit your children. Decorate shoe boxes and fill them with toiletries for people who are moving into transitional housing. Take cookies to a retirement community or perform a show for the people who live there. Or, your entire family can participate in a walk together to raise money and awareness for an issue or charity. There are so many opportunities to give to others who will really appreciate your efforts.

- **Set an example of giving.** Take dinner to a friend who just had a baby; give cold drinks to the trash collectors and say "thank you." By showing them how good it feels to give to others, you are emphasizing all the things that you and your children have and how fortunate you all are. This will help them realize the many ways that *they* can give to others. They'll catch on and follow your lead.

- **Reinforce the value of giving from the heart.** Suggest giving handmade gifts rather than store bought ones. Your children can make necklaces for girlfriends and grandmas, frame a piece of their artwork for Dad's or Mom's office, make a sticker collection box or create a coupon book listing household chores that they will do for their siblings. Often, the best gifts are those that can't be purchased in a store.

- **Make giving a part of your family's lifestyle.** There are so many ways that you and your family can regularly give to others in need. Even at the youngest age, children can search through closets and toy chests providing wonderful opportunities to learn to give to others in need. There are clothing drives, food drives, and book drives in most communities throughout the year. It's a great feeling to be a part of helping those in your community that are in need. These simple, but regular avenues of giving reinforce the importance of helping others as part of your family dynamic.

Teaching children to care about others is a true gift. It helps builds self-esteem and self-worth. They begin to believe that their actions matter, that they can make a difference in their world by making a difference in the lives of others. And, while the holiday season does provide a perfect example -- every day is filled with opportunities to teach the value of giving from the heart!

Interactive Family Art Activity
Make "Thanks for Being Special to Me" Cards

You can help your children make "Gratitude Gifts" – just like CiCi and Ace did -- for all the special people in their lives. Remember that not everyone on your child's list has to receive the same gift. The important thing is that you help your children communicate their feelings of gratitude at the holiday season.

Before you start the project, ask your children to make a list of all the people they are thankful for having in their lives. Tell them that you are going to help them make gifts for special friends and relatives to say thank you for all the nice things they do all year. Encourage them to think of people that would really appreciate a "thank you" at this time of year like teachers, doctors, babysitters, neighbors, mail carriers ...anyone who makes their lives a little nicer, a little happier.

You will need:

- **Construction paper in different colors or card stock from the craft store**
- **Paints and rubber stamps**
- **Markers or crayons**
- **Stickers, glitter, ribbons**
- **Glue or tape**
- **Whatever else you want to use to decorate your cards.**

1 Fold your construction paper in half, making a card. You can cut patterns along the edges or just leave them straight. Or, you can make the whole card in a shape, like a heart or a diamond. Be creative; it's all up to you.

2 Design special pictures with paints, glitter, stickers, markers or using rubber stamps...or any other decorative touches you want to add. Each card should be unique, just like the people you are giving them to. For example, you can draw a picture of you holding hands with your best friend on one card, paint a rainbow on another, or make an animal and sticker collage on another.

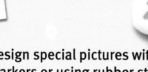

3 Write your message inside to say "thank you" for the nice things each person does to make your life so wonderful. Each card should reflect something that makes that person special to you. Ask your children to write or dictate to you something they are thankful for about each friend, teacher, and relative or community helper.

Every time that you share, you show someone special that you care.
When they receive these cards from you,
you're saying "thanks" for all they do.

Remember that these creations are your children's ways of sharing parts of themselves with the special people in their lives. Don't forget to tell them how special they are to you and how proud you are of their sharing and giving!

For other ideas for "Gratitude Gifts," please visit us @ **childrensplace.com**. Shimmering snowflakes to decorate doors, a "Special Things" Box for someone special, Bountiful Birdie treats, and other projects to do together are all waiting online. Come enjoy together.

The Greatest Gift

What can I give to you to show you
how much you mean to me?
What can I do or what can I say?
How can I make you see?

I'd give you sunshine everyday,
blow all the clouds away
for clear blue skies and butterflies.
I'd send them all your way.

I'd wish you giggles and smiles
all day long, and in your heart,
I hope you'll always have a song.
I wish you happiness and laughter, too.
These things I'd wish for you.

And, Love...Love!
Love...Love!
Oh, yes, I'd wish you Love!

There's Mom, Dad
and my whole family;
they love me whatever I do.
Doctors and teachers and so many more
who help to take care of you.

I'd give you thanks with kisses and hugs.
I'd give you dances by lightning bugs
that light up the sky when they go by
and teach you how to fly.

I'd give you the bright sun
and moon above and sprinkle them
with stars of love.
I'd wish you rainbow days
and sweet dreams, too.
These things I'd wish for you.

And, Love...Love!
Love...Love!
Oh, yes, I'd wish you Love!

What can I give to you?
What can I say or do?
You give so much to me.
How can I make you see?
What can I do?

I'd give you wishes on shooting stars,
and your very own race cars.
I'd give you my hand
so you'd understand
I'm with you wherever you are.

I'd wish you happy times
and lots of friends,
a smile on your face
when your day ends.
I'd give you everything
you'd wish for too.
I'd wish it back for you.

And Love...Love!
Love...Love!
Oh, yes, I'd give you Love!

And Love...Love!
Love...Love!
Oh, yes, I'd give you Love!

Just Make A Wish!

Last night I dreamed I was a fairy
floating through the sky.
I dreamed I was in a race car
really zoomin' by.
Yes, anything you want to dream
is right inside your head.
So, close your eyes.
Dream with me.
And, hop right into bed.

Just make a wish.
Make a wish, make a wish, you see.
(Ba-duba-dup)
Anything you want to be.
(Ba-duba-dup)
'Cause in your dreams,
it's all up to you.
(Ba-duba-dup)
What you want to be or do.

Anywhere you want to go,
or anything you want to know,
it's all inside your dreams, you see.
So, close your eyes and dream with me.

Anytime, night or day,
dreams are there for you to play.
Think of something you want to be.
Then, dream your dream,
and you will see.

Just make a wish.
Make a wish, make a wish, you see.
(Ba-duba-dup)
Anything you want to be.
(Ba-duba-dup)
Doesn't matter who you are,
(Ba-duba-dup)
or even if there's no star.

Dreams can come true
'cause they're a part of you.
So, anything you want to be,
just close your eyes and you will see.

In your dreams,
you can be
anything you want to be.
Racin' cars, fly on shootin' stars
or meetin' friends on planet Mars.